A GOLDEN BOOK • NEW YORK

Andy was a very lucky boy. He had lots of different **toys**. But his favorite toy was a cowboy named **Woody**.

Andy loved to
play with Woody.

But there was something Andy didn't know about Woody and the other toys. When Andy wasn't around, the toys had a life of their own. They **moved**. They **talked**. They **laughed**. And they had **adventures**.

All toys did. But only when no one was **watching**.

One year, Andy got a brand-new toy for his birthday—a space ranger named **Buzz Lightyear**! Buzz had flashing **lasers, gadgets,** and even **wings.**

Buzz thought he was a
real space ranger. He
even thought he could **fly**!
Woody tried to tell Buzz
that he was actually a toy.
But Buzz wouldn't listen.

Soon Buzz became Andy's new favorite toy.
This made Woody very **sad**.

One day, Andy was going to Pizza Planet. His mom told him he could bring just one toy. Woody wanted to go! He tried to shove Buzz aside. But he accidentally pushed Buzz out Andy's bedroom **window** instead. **Whoops!**

Woody got to go with Andy, but the other toys were very **upset**. They thought Woody had pushed Buzz out the window on purpose.

Woody felt bad—
until Buzz turned up in
the car, too!

Buzz was **angry** with Woody. The two began to fight.
When the car stopped at a gas station, they tumbled
out the back door.

Oh, no! Andy and his mom drove off to Pizza Planet, leaving Buzz and Woody behind. They had become **lost toys!** And Andy's family was moving to a new home in just two days.

Then Woody spotted a
Pizza Planet truck. Woody
told Buzz the truck was a
spaceship, and they hopped
on board.

Buzz insisted on riding
up front. Luckily, a
stack of pizza boxes
kept him hidden
from the driver.

At Pizza Planet, Buzz climbed into a claw game filled with **toy aliens**. Buzz thought the game was a **spaceship**.

Woody tried to get Buzz out—but soon they were both trapped!

Oh, no! Andy's mean neighbor, **Sid**, captured Buzz and Woody. Sid loved to torture toys. Woody and Buzz were in **trouble**! Sid took Buzz and Woody home with him.

Sid's room was full of **mutant toys**. He had created them by combining different toy parts in strange ways . . . and now he had evil plans for Buzz and Woody! They had to escape.

Buzz tried to **fly** out of Sid's house, but he fell. He finally realized that Woody was right—he wasn't a real space ranger. He was only a **toy**.

Sid strapped a **rocket** to Buzz. He planned to blow Buzz to pieces! Buzz and Woody had to work **together** if they were going to escape.

But Buzz didn't want to escape. He felt sad because he wasn't a real space ranger. Woody helped Buzz understand that Andy loved him and that being a **toy** was very important.

And before they knew it, Buzz and Woody had become **friends**.

Woody came up with a plan to save Buzz. He asked **Sid's toys** to help. Just as Sid was about to **blow** Buzz up, Woody and the mutant toys came to life. Sid was **terrified**—he screamed and ran away!

Buzz and Woody were thrilled! So were Sid's toys. They knew that Sid would never torture them again.

Now Buzz and Woody were free to go back to Andy. But Andy's moving van was already pulling away from his house. They had to catch up to it!

Buzz and Woody ran and ran. Sid's mean dog, **Scud**, began to **chase** them!

Luckily, RC came out of the moving van to give Buzz and Woody a ride. They thought they were home free—until RC's batteries began to run down!

Then they remembered that Buzz still had Sid's **rocket** strapped to his back. Woody launched it. **WHOOSH!** Buzz, Woody, and RC flew through the air. RC landed safely in the back of the moving van. But Buzz and Woody kept going.

Buzz popped open his **wings**. The rocket flew into the air and exploded. Buzz and Woody were **falling**! But thanks to Buzz's wings, they were falling with style. Buzz held on to Woody and veered toward **Andy's car**.

Buzz and Woody glided through the car's **sunroof** and plopped down next to **Andy**—right where they belonged.

Do **you** like toys?

Well, Andy sure does. He has all different kinds of toys, and he loves to play with each and every one of them.

But Andy's favorite toys are a cowboy
named Woody . . .

. . . and a space ranger named
Buzz Lightyear!

One day, something terrible happened.

Woody was **toynapped**!

You see, Woody wasn't just a toy. He was a **FAMOUS** toy who once had his own TV show.

Along with Jessie the cowgirl, Bullseye the horse, and Stinky Pete the prospector, Woody starred in *Woody's Roundup.*

Because Woody and the other *Roundup* toys were so famous, Al, a greedy toy store owner, was going to sell them to a museum—all the way across the world in **Japan**!

Jessie, Bullseye, and the Prospector were very excited. They had been in **STORAGE** for a long time.

But Woody didn't want to go to a silly **museum**! He wanted to go back home to Andy!

That is, he did until Jessie told him a story.

Just as Woody had Andy, Jessie once had a little girl who loved her.

They played together.

They laughed together.

They spent every day
together—until the girl grew
up and forgot all about Jessie.

Woody began to wonder if Andy
would grow up and forget about him.
Maybe the museum wouldn't be so bad after all. . . .

Meanwhile, Buzz Lightyear had been busy planning a rescue mission.

Mr. Potato Head,

Slinky Dog,

Hamm,

Buzz,

and **Rex**

all set off together
to find Woody.

To get to Al's Toy Barn, the
toys had to cross a busy street.
Fortunately, they had a plan.

Success!

Inside the store, Buzz and the others had to face another challenge—a new (and confused) Buzz Lightyear toy.

And little did they know that an evil toy named Emperor Zurg was hot on their trail!

But **nothing** would stop Buzz and his friends from finding Woody!

They quickly found Al in the office of the toy store and followed him to his apartment— and there was Woody!

But there was one **problem**.

Woody had decided to go to the museum with the other *Roundup* toys. He didn't want to end up **forgotten** and in **storage**.

Buzz tried to convince Woody to go home
to Andy, but the cowboy had made up his mind.
So Buzz and the others left—without Woody.

It didn't take Woody long to realize that he had made a mistake. His true place was with Andy, not in a museum!

But the Prospector had a different plan. He was going to the museum, and no **cowboy** would stand in his way. He trapped Woody, Jessie, and Bullseye in the apartment. Then Al took them away.

Woody's friends had to rescue him, but first they had to defeat **Zurg**!

Now they had to hurry—Al was on his way to the airport. Next stop, **Japan**!

Buzz Lightyear to the **rescue**! Buzz, Mr. Potato Head, Hamm, Rex, and Slinky borrowed a car and raced to the airport.

They rescued Woody
and Bullseye—
and sent the
Prospector packing!

Unfortunately,
poor Jessie got
stuck on the plane!

Would Woody and Buzz be able to save her?

Of course they would!

Yee-haa!

Soon Woody, Buzz, Rex, Hamm, Mr. Potato Head, and Slinky were back in Andy's room— along with their new friends, Jessie and Bullseye!

All the toys knew they couldn't stop Andy from growing up—but they wouldn't miss it for the world!

Disney · PIXAR

TOY STORY 3

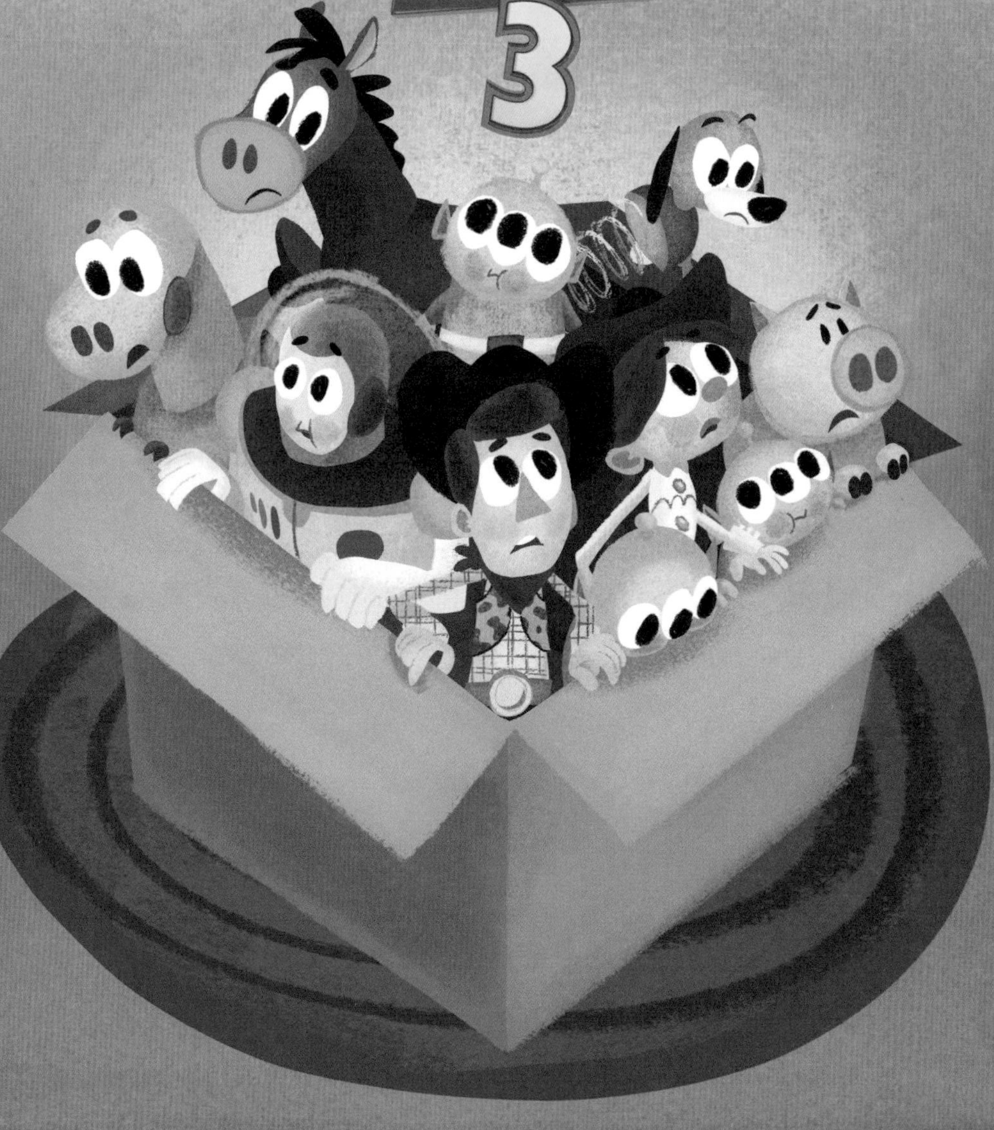

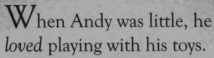

When Andy was little, he *loved* playing with his toys. There were **Rex**, **Hamm**, **Jessie**, **Bullseye**, **Buzz Lightyear**, **Slinky Dog**, **the Aliens** . . .

. . . and Andy's very favorite toy—**Sheriff Woody**.

Now Andy has **GROWN UP** and is packing for college. He is going to take Woody with him.

Andy plans to store his other toys in the attic.
But Andy's mom picks up the bag by mistake.
Oh, no! She thinks it's trash!

Luckily, the toys avoid the garbage truck. They make a daring **E/CAPE** to the garage!

Woody explains that it was a big mistake—Andy didn't mean to throw them away. But no one believes him.

Jessie spots a donation box, and the toys climb in.

The box of toys gets donated to Sunnyside Daycare. Jessie, Buzz, and the gang are thrilled! They find **cheerful toys** and all the **extra batteries** they could want!

Lots-o'-Huggin' Bear welcomes the new toys warmly. "Being donated was the best thing that ever happened to you!" says Lotso. "You'll never be outgrown or forgotten."

Woody still doesn't think
they belong there. "We're
Andy's toys," he says. He
leaves for home by himself.

He uses a kite to go **UP**!

Then he goes **DOWN**!

A little girl named
Bonnie finds Woody
and takes him
to her house.

Back at Sunnyside, things are not so sunny.
The daycare children **THROW**, *SMASH*,
and *SLOBBER ON* the toys.

Everyone feels **ACHY** and **HURT**. Woody was right—they don't belong here. The toys need help! They want to go back to Andy.

That night, Buzz goes to talk to Lotso.

But there is one more big problem. . . .

It's **Lotso**! He wants Andy's toys to stay with the toddlers who haven't learned to play nicely with toys yet. That's so the toddlers won't play with *him*!

Lotso gets his toughest friends to capture Buzz. The space ranger is in trouble!

The other toys are in trouble, too!
Lotso locks them in **jail** for the night . . .
and Buzz is the guard! Lotso has pressed a button
on Buzz. The space ranger now believes that
Andy's toys are **enemies** working for the evil
Emperor Zurg!

Meanwhile, Woody is having fun at Bonnie's house. He meets nice toys.

An old clown named Chuckles says that he knew Lotso a long time ago. Woody learns that Lotso is bad—and his friends are in **DANGER**!

Woody wants to go home to Andy, but his friends need **help**!

Woody sneaks back into Sunnyside. The toys **PLAN** their escape.

Woody and Slinky **GRAB** the daycare keys!

It's time to **RE/ET** Buzz.

The toys sneak
across the playground.
Shhh!

"This is the only
way out," says Woody.

Oh, no! Lotso is waiting at the Dumpster.

The toys struggle to get past Lotso. But a garbage truck arrives. Now everyone is headed for the **garbage dump**!

At the dump, the toys are **PUSHED** onto
a conveyor belt. They're moving toward the
incinerator! The toys are scared, but
everyone sticks together.

The toys give Lotso a boost so he can reach the **STOP** button. But Lotso changes his mind . . . and *doesn't* push the button!

"**N**_O_O_O.!"

yells Woody as he and the other toys come closer to the fire.

Suddenly, a huge claw **SCOOPS** the toys up. The Aliens have saved their friends!

Lotso finds a new home . . .

. . . while the toys return to their old one.
But Woody knows that things will never
be like they used to be. Andy has grown up.
Then Woody has an **idea**.

At first, Andy isn't sure he wants to give away his toys. But when he meets Bonnie, he knows they will be

LOVED.

Woody and Buzz watch as Andy
drives away.

"So long, partner," says Woody.
Although Woody will miss his friend,
Andy will always have a special place
in his

heart.